THE LOST DOLL

Emily was heartbroken when she lost
her very special rag doll in the park.
But she was sure that
somehow it could be found—
even in a big city....

A warm, satisfying story about
the "human" side of city life.

"But she's not just a doll," Emily burst out. *"She's Agnes."*

THE LOST DOLL

STORY BY
PEGGY MANN

PICTURES BY
THOMAS DI GRAZIA

RANDOM HOUSE ⌂ NEW YORK

Text copyright © 1972 by Peggy Mann
Illustrations copyright © 1972 by Thomas di Grazia
All rights reserved under International and Pan-American
Copyright Conventions. Published in the United States
by Random House, Inc., New York, and simultaneously
in Canada by Random House of Canada Limited, Toronto.

Library of Congress Cataloging in Publication Data

Mann, Peggy.
    The lost doll.

    SUMMARY: With the help of a number of city
officials, Emily finds her very special lost rag doll.
    [1. Dolls—Fiction] I. Di Grazia, Thomas, illus.
II. Title.
PZ7.M31513Lo   813'.5'4 [Fic]
78-37412   ISBN 0-394-82104-1
ISBN 0-394-92104-6 (lib. bdg.)

Manufactured in the United States of America

For my daughter Betsy
and *her* Agnes

Contents

THE LOST DOLL

THE SURPRISE PRESENT

"What could it *be?*" said Emily as she hung up the telephone.

She turned to her mother. "Grandma has a present for me. She's bringing it tomorrow."

"Yes," her mother said, smiling. "I know."

"You know what it *is?*"

Her mother nodded.

"Please!" said Emily.

"Uh uh!" said her mother. "You'll never get me to tell. So don't even try."

Emily did try anyway. But it was no use. All that her mother would do was shake her head. And smile.

It must be something very special, Emily decided. Maybe it was—oh, she *hoped* it was—a very special doll. A doll which spoke real sentences when you pulled a string. Or a doll which crawled around the floor when you pressed a secret button. Or a doll which could roller-skate.

There were so many wonderful things a doll could do. She had seen them all advertised on TV.

Maybe Grandma was bringing her a doll which could do *everything!*

The box was big. Just the right size to hold a very special doll. "Oh, Grandma!" Emily exclaimed, so excited she could hardly speak. "How come you're giving me a present? It's not even my birthday or Christmas or *any*thing! So how come?"

"Just because," Grandma said. (She seemed excited herself.)

"Because *what?*" Emily demanded.

"Because I love you, that's what," Grandma said.

Carefully Emily took off the fancy giftwrappings. Then she closed her eyes, held her breath, and lifted the lid off the box.

She opened her eyes.

It was a doll, all right.

But *what* a doll! A stupid, floppy rag doll—which couldn't do anything at all. It didn't even look

real. It looked, in fact, like something Grandma had *made.*

"I made her myself," Grandma said, sounding very proud. "Do you like her?"

Emily nodded.

"Do you *really?*" Grandma asked, sounding a little worried now.

"Oh, yes," Emily replied politely. "I do. She's very nice."

Grandma sat on the couch and held the doll on her knees. "I rather like her myself," she announced. "She reminds me of a rag doll I had when I was a little girl. I called her Agnes. I slept with her every single night."

Emily looked at her grandmother with sudden interest. Somehow she had never thought of Grandma as ever having been a little girl. She tried to imagine it. But she couldn't. All she could see was a tiny Grandma sitting on the couch holding some stupid rag doll. Named Agnes.

When Grandma left, Emily threw the rag doll on top of the toy chest. "What on earth good are *you?*" she said.

The doll just sat there smiling its silly stitched-on smile.

Practically *every* doll at least had eyes which opened and closed. This doll didn't. Its eyes were black buttons.

6

Most dolls had hair you could at least wash if you wanted to. This doll didn't. *Her* hair was made out of old brown yarn, left over, Grandma had said, from the sweater she knitted for Grandpa's birthday.

Most dolls could be given a bath. Not *this* one. *She* was made out of a linen dishtowel; stuffed with down from one of Grandma's old sofa pillows.

Lots of dolls could at least suck a bottle and wet their diapers. But not *this* doll.

This doll couldn't do *any*thing. Except smile.

AGNES

For the next few days Emily scarcely looked at the rag doll. Instead, she played school with her stuffed animals. She dressed and undressed her teenage doll, which had a trunkful of clothes and one leg missing. And she played with her farm game, setting out the animals in separate pastures on the rug.

All that time the rag doll just sat on the toy chest, smiling.

Once Emily shouted at her, "What are you smiling at, you stupid?"

Another time she stuck out her tongue at the rag doll.

8

Finally, she took it by one leg and slung it into her closet. Then she slammed the closet door closed.

She was cross at the doll—for making her so disappointed.

But that night, in bed, Emily thought of the little rag doll lying on the closet floor. She began to feel guilty. After all, it wasn't the doll's fault that it couldn't do anything.

Presently Emily got out of bed and opened the closet door. She got down on her hands and knees and felt around on the closet floor. Had the doll disappeared?

Quickly she put on the bedtable lamp, and went back to look again.

There it was. It had fallen partway into Emily's high, black rainboot.

"I'm . . . sorry," Emily said.

She brought it back to bed with her. Then she raised her knees into a hill and sat the doll on top.

The rag doll smiled in a very cheerful way.

Emily smiled back. "I may as well give you a name," she said. "I'll call you Agnes."

She began to braid Agnes' hair. Whenever she got a new doll she always redid the hairstyle. There wasn't too much that could be done with hair made out of strands of brown yarn. But at least Agnes' hair could be braided every night and unbraided again in the morning.

"I guess Grandma must have worked pretty

hard on you," Emily said. "Sewing each separate piece of hair into your head."

She waggled Agnes' head; the doll nodded in agreement.

Then Emily noticed Agnes' underwear. The panties had tiny frills of lace around the legs. And the slip was made in several layers, so that Agnes' skirt would stick out in a perky way.

"It must have taken Grandma a long time," Emily said. "Sewing all those tiny little stitches." Once Emily had made a cape for her panda bear. She had tried her best to make little stitches, so she knew how hard it was. And after a day all her stitches had come undone.

"You don't have to worry," she said to Agnes. "*Your* stitches will never come undone. Grandma sewed you very, very well."

Agnes smiled, and Emily settled the doll beside her on the pillow.

She remembered how Grandma had said: *She reminds me of a rag doll I had when I was a little girl. I called her Agnes. I slept with her every single night.*

"Would you like to sleep with *me* every night?" Emily asked.

Agnes smiled.

Emily smiled back. "Okay," she said. Somehow it made her feel good—doing the very same thing Grandma had done in the old-fashioned days.

Then, suddenly, she understood something. Grandma had once had a doll exactly like this— which she loved. And Grandma had gone to all the trouble to make *this* doll because she loved Emily. So Agnes was, after all, a very special doll.

LOST

The next morning before she went to school Emily phoned her grandmother.

"Hi, Grandma," she said. "I just want to tell you . . . I *love* the doll you made me. I named her Agnes."

"Why—how nice of you to call me, Em!" Grandma sounded surprised, and very pleased.

"I'm going to sleep with her every single night," said Emily. "Just like you did, Grandma."

"Would you like me to make her a little nightgown?" Grandma asked.

"Oh," said Emily, "that would be wonderful."

As it turned out, Emily not only took Agnes to bed with her. Sometimes she took her to school too, and other daytime places.

Grandma made a special little carrying bag for the doll. And Emily would pop Agnes into it when she went visiting . . . or shopping with Mother . . . or to the movies. Agnes *loved* movies.

One afternoon Emily went to the park with her friend Joe who lived down the street. She took Agnes along.

Joe liked to climb rocks. But it was hard for Emily to climb with a doll dangling from her arm. So she left Agnes sitting at the bottom of the rocks. "You stay there like a good girl," she said. "Don't move. I'll be right back."

But, as Emily and Joe reached the top of the rock-mountain, a huge, spotted dog suddenly sprang out at them, barking fiercely.

The children screamed. They scrambled down the rocks, and ran back to Joe's mother.

"People who bring dogs to the park should keep them on leashes," said Joe's mother. She sounded very cross. "Come on. Let's get out of here. It's time to go home, anyway."

So they left the park quickly. And in the excitement, Emily forgot all about Agnes.

The big spotted dog saw Agnes. He came bounding down the rocks and pounced on her. Then

he shook her up and carried her off—straight across the park. Finally, he dropped her in the bushes. For a while he barked at her fiercely. But since Agnes simply lay there, the dog quickly lost interest. He turned and trotted away.

Soon a boy playing Indian all by himself discovered the little rag doll. Letting out a loud Indian war whoop, he grabbed Agnes and took her prisoner. "I'm gonna *scalp* you!" he cried. He pulled at her hair. But it was sewn in too well. It wouldn't come out. So he decided to take Agnes home and scalp her with his boy-scout knife.

He stuck the doll into his pocket. But on his way across the street, Agnes fell out.

She lay smiling up at the sky.

A taxi came charging at her. Though it passed over her body like a moving tunnel, the wheels did not touch her.

Then a green bus came lumbering along. Closer. *Closer!* It was just about to roll over Agnes when——

——the red traffic lights popped on. The bus drew to a halt, with one great black wheel just inches from the doll. When the bus started moving again, there would be no escape. The huge and heavy bus would crush Agnes!

People started hurrying across the street. Among them came a mother pushing a stroller. The baby spied Agnes. "I want dat!" he cried.

The mother looked down. Seeing that Agnes was about to be run over, she scooped her up and hurried on across the street. When they reached the other side, she sat Agnes on a wooden bench by the East Side entrance to the park.

"I WANT dat!" the baby shouted.

"No, David," his mother said. "It might be dirty. Besides, some little girl will probably come looking for it." She continued on to the playground. But all the way the baby kept screaming, "I want dat!"

Agnes sat there alone on the park bench, staring out at the people who passed by.

THE SEARCH

Emily, of course, did not forget about her doll for long. As soon as she got home she cried out in a loud remembering voice, "AGNES!"

But Emily's mother was bathing the baby. Then she had to fix dinner. So *she* couldn't go back to the park to look for Agnes. And when Daddy got home, dinner was all ready. So *he* couldn't go out to get Agnes.

Emily scarcely ate anything. She was much too worried.

"Please!" she begged, as soon as dinner was over. "Oh, *please!* Won't *somebody* take me out now to look for my doll?"

So Daddy did.

Darkness was settling over the city. But Daddy had brought a flashlight.

"I know exactly where I left her!" Emily exclaimed. "Right by the big rocks." She pulled at Daddy's hand to hurry him along. When they reached the rocks, she pointed. "Shine your light right *there,* Dad."

Daddy did. The light glinted on a broken pop bottle and some stubbly grass.

Emily swallowed hard. "I *know* this is where she was." Tears stung her eyes.

"Maybe you left her on the other side of the rocks," Daddy said. He walked around, shining the flashlight here, there, everywhere.

But no Agnes.

Emily tripped over a rock, fell down, scraped her knee. She began to cry.

"There's no use stumbling around here in the dark," Daddy said. "We'll try again tomorrow. Don't cry, Em."

But Emily couldn't stop. She kept on crying all the way home.

That night—for the first time in weeks—Emily went to bed without Agnes.

But she couldn't sleep. After a while she sat up and called, "Mom-m-m-e-e-e!"

Her mother came in. "Aren't you asleep *yet?*"

"If *I* was lost," Emily demanded, "what would *you* do?"

"I'd phone the police."

"Then phone them about Agnes," said Emily.

"Well," her mother said, "the police are pretty busy these days. I don't know if they'd bother themselves about a doll."

"But she's not just a doll," Emily burst out. "She's *Agnes.*"

"Tell you what," her mother said, "tomorrow—if you don't find Agnes in the park—Daddy will take you to the police station. Maybe someone will have turned her in. Now you lie down, Em, and go to sleep. Worrying won't help you find your doll."

THE POLICE

At six o'clock the next morning Emily woke her father.

"What's the big idea!" he grumbled. "It's *Saturday*. I always sleep late on Saturday morning. Remember?"

"Agnes!" Emily said in a very loud whisper.

"But not so *early!*" Daddy groaned.

"It's daylight," Emily insisted. "Someone may find her and steal her. *Please*, Daddy."

Her daddy gave Emily a long look. Then he muttered something under his breath and got up.

They were the only ones in that part of the park.

They looked on top of the rocks. And beneath the rocks. And behind the rocks. And between the rocks.

But no use.

No Agnes.

So they went along to the 24th Precinct police station. They left the park by the West Side entrance. Agnes was still sitting on a bench by the East Side entrance. So, of course, they did not see her.

Officer Tom at the 24th Precinct was as efficient as any policeman on television. And he was very nice. Though he didn't have Agnes, he filled out a form about her.

"If someone brings her in," he told Emily, "we'll let you know right away. You can come pick her up."

"What if she's brought in to some *other* police station?" Emily asked.

"Then," said Officer Tom, "*they* will notify the Police Department's Lost Property Unit. Lost Property will take down the details. And when you telephone them, they'll let you know which police station has Agnes."

He wrote down the telephone number—964-2313—and handed it to Emily.

"I'll call them every single day!" she declared.

MISS PICKERING

At ten o'clock that same morning, an old lady sat down on the bench by the East Side entrance to the park. She came there every day after breakfast to get some fresh air and read the newspaper.

She opened her large, black pocketbook, put on her reading spectacles, looked up—and saw Agnes.

"Well!" she exclaimed. "Who have we here?"

She took Agnes onto her lap. The doll was slightly damp from the morning dew. But the old lady did not mind. "You know," she said, "you remind me of a doll I used to have when I was a child."

She propped Agnes next to her on the bench.

"If no one comes to claim you by the time I'm ready to leave," she said, "I think I'll adopt you!"

No one came.

The old lady felt rather relieved. As she sat reading her newspaper, she had cast little glances at Agnes. And the doll had smiled at her cheerfully. "You're company, and that's a fact," the old lady said. And when she left the park, she popped Agnes into her large, black pocketbook.

On the way home she passed a policeman. For just a second she hesitated—then hurried on. "What good to give this doll to a policeman!" she told herself. "It would only sit unclaimed in some Lost and Found."

Then another voice inside her said, "But this doll must belong to some little girl who loves her very much."

The old lady stopped. She opened her purse and looked inside. The doll lay there smiling up at her sweetly.

The old lady smiled back.

Suddenly she was in her girlhood again, looking down at her own rag doll.

"Those were happier days," she said softly. "And that's a fact."

She snapped her pocketbook closed.

"I *need* this little doll," she told herself. "I was *meant* to find it. Otherwise, why would it have been sitting right there—on my park bench?"

The old lady took Agnes home to the room where she lived, all alone. It was a crowded room. There were piles of newspapers in the corner, unwashed dishes in the sink, and framed photographs on the bureau, the table top, and the walls. She kept these photographs to remind her of happier days.

"Now where shall I put you, dear?" she said, taking Agnes from the pocketbook. "Perhaps high up on the bureau so you can see everything. . . . All right?"

Agnes smiled.

"My name is Ida Pickering," the old lady said. "Ida M. Pickering. M. for Muriel. I wonder what *your* name is."

Agnes stared back with her black-button eyes.

"Well, we'll think of a nice *new* name for you," Miss Pickering said. She put the doll on the bureau top, and propped her up against a container of Epsom salts.

Agnes sat there, staring out at the small and crowded room.

"AGNES, WHERE ARE YOU?"

The front door banged closed.

Emily was home from school.

Before she even took off her coat, she ran to the telephone and dialed the number of the Police Department's Lost Property Unit. She did this every afternoon. And every afternoon the answers were the same.

"I'm sorry, no."

"Not yet, young lady."

"Nope. No one's sent in a report about a rag doll."

Finally, after three weeks, Emily's mother said, "Look, dear, if the doll hasn't been turned in yet, I really doubt you'll ever find her."

"I *will!*" Emily insisted. But secretly she had lost all hope. In this whole huge city—a place crowded with busy people—how could anyone expect to track down one little doll?

"Look," her mother said, "Grandma can make you another rag doll. Exactly like Agnes."

"But she won't *be* Agnes!" Emily wailed. "And *I don't want her!*"

After a long moment her mother said, "Well, suppose you try telephoning for one more week. But then, if they *still* have no word about Agnes, you'll just have to forget about her. Agreed?"

"All right," Emily said. "I'll stop telephoning. But I won't forget about Agnes. How *could* I?"

For one more week she telephoned. She knew the number by heart. She also knew by heart the answers she would receive.

"I'm sorry, young lady."
"Nope."
"No report on a rag doll."

Then—as she had promised—Emily stopped telephoning. But she did not even *try* to forget about Agnes.

She could have put one of her other dolls, or even a stuffed animal, in Agnes' special daytime place—on the pillow of her bed. And she could have slept with another doll or stuffed animal at night. But she never did. It would only have made her miss Agnes all the more.

Often, in bed at night, Emily would say right out loud, "Agnes, where *are* you? You must be *some-*where! Oh, Agnes, what has *happened* to you?"

AGNES TAKES A TRIP

All that time Agnes was sitting on the top of the old lady's bureau, propped up by the box of Epsom salts.

Miss Pickering often spoke to the doll, consulted her about various things. "Which TV program should we watch?" . . . "How cold do you s'pose it is out? Should I wear my black coat or will that be too heavy?" . . . "Now what shall we have for vegetables? Carrots and peas? Or squash?"

The doll just sat there staring out with her black-button eyes. It seemed that she was thinking about other things.

After a while the old lady began to grow annoyed with the little doll—though she didn't quite know why.

She had never given Agnes a name. She called her simply "Dear" or, sometimes, "Sweetie."

"You probably have a name already," Miss Pickering had said once as she took Agnes up and looked straight into her eyes. "If only I knew what it was."

Strangely enough, the doll did not bring to Miss Pickering memories of happier days. Instead, for some reason, she made Miss Pickering feel rather . . . sad. Or guilty.

Often when she looked at the rag doll Miss Pickering wondered about the little girl the doll had belonged to. Had the child loved this doll very much? Was she still looking for her little rag doll?

Somehow the doll seemed rather lost and alone as she sat high on the bureau top. She never looked as though she belonged here in Ida M. Pickering's room.

One afternoon Miss Pickering put on her new blue dress. It was time for her monthly visit to her nephew and his wife and her little grandniece Doreen. They invited her to dinner the first Sunday of every month. Miss Pickering looked forward to these Sundays. She loved her nephew and his wife, and especially her little niece Doreen.

As Miss Pickering passed the bureau, she suddenly stopped and looked hard at Agnes. "You *don't* belong here!" she said. "And that's a fact. Dolls were meant for little girls to *play* with. Not to sit, day after day, in a room where an old lady lives all alone. I know what I shall do with you. I'll give you to my niece Doreen."

When Miss Pickering left the room, Agnes went with her—shut inside the big, black pocketbook.

As usual, Miss Pickering took the subway to her brother's house. As usual, she read her newspaper. Then, as usual, when she had finished the paper she looked at all the advertisements posted around the subway car.

There was one advertisement which was not usual at all. In fact, she had never noticed it before.

An Auction Sale of Unclaimed Articles in the Lost Property Office of the New York City Transit System will be held at the South End of the SUBWAY CONCOURSE *at J Street (Boro Hall Station) of the Independent Division at 9:30* A.M. *on April 10th. Auctioneer: Mr. H. Phillips.*

An auction—of unclaimed articles!

Miss Pickering read the advertisement through three times. Each time she read it she felt more and more excited.

Perhaps the little girl who had lost her rag doll

would read this advertisement too. Perhaps she would go to the auction, hoping her doll might be there. And what if she actually found her doll there! What a reunion there would be!

Miss Pickering found herself smiling as she thought about it.

Suddenly she thought again of her own rag doll which she had loved as a little girl. She remembered the doll's name. Annie. That was it—Annie! A wave of happiness went through her as she remembered the love she had felt for Annie, so long ago.

Somehow she felt very certain that the doll in her pocketbook was loved by some little girl somewhere just as much as she had loved her Annie.

When she got off the subway, Miss Pickering walked up to the change booth. She snapped open her pocketbook and took out the rag doll. She shoved it across the small counter to the man in the change booth. "This," she said, "is for the subway auction of unclaimed articles."

Then she hurried away.

But the man called to her, "Hey, lady. Come back here."

Miss Pickering turned, looking a little surprised. "Me?" she said. She went back to the change booth.

"We need some information," the man said. "Your name. Address. When you found this doll. And where."

"Oh, dear," said Miss Pickering. Then, in a soft, ashamed voice she confessed that she had not found the doll in the subway. "Does that mean," she asked, "that you won't accept her for the subway auction?"

"We'll accept her, lady," the change-booth man said, "no matter where you found her. But I've got to fill out this ticket for her, so please, lady, answer the questions I asked you."

Miss Pickering answered the questions.

The change-booth man filled out a ticket, and tied it to Agnes' arm.

"I do hope you find your owner, dear," Miss Pickering said.

Then, quickly, she hurried away from the little rag doll.

AGNES' ADVENTURES

For hours Agnes sat at the barred window of the change booth, smiling out at people as they stopped to buy their subway tokens. Many of the people smiled back at Agnes.

At midnight there was a knock on the locked door of the change booth.

"At last!" the change-booth man said. He unlocked the door and a short, dark man came in—the lunch-relief man. He was carrying a large, bulging canvas bag.

"Sorry to be so long, Mike," the lunch-relief man said.

41

"I'm sitting here slowly starving to death," the change-booth man said.

"Well, who's your girl friend?" the lunch-relief man asked. He picked up Agnes and winked at her. Then he read the ticket tied to her arm.

"See you in an hour," the change-booth man said. "I'm off for my roast beef on rye."

The lunch-relief man dumped Agnes into his large canvas bag. As she landed—on her head—a sharp umbrella spike poked her in the stomach. There were other lost items in the bag, collected by the lunch-relief man at other change booths: a wallet, a woolen glove, a baseball bat—and the umbrella.

After what seemed like a very long time the change-booth man returned. And the lunch-relief man left. He slung his bag of lost items over his shoulder. Then he took the subway.

He got off at the 179th Street station, and went into the dispatcher's office.

"Well," he said, throwing his canvas bag on the table, "here's today's haul. Be seein' you, Sam." And he hurried off.

The dispatcher emptied Agnes, the wallet, the glove, the baseball bat, and the umbrella into a larger canvas bag in which there were many other lost items. Then he closed the bag, and locked it.

At four that morning, while almost everyone in the city slept, a special subway car drew into the

179th Street station. The canvas bag in which Agnes lay was slung aboard. There were eight revenue agents on that subway car. Each wore a uniform. Each had a gun. There were also two policemen.

All these uniformed men had not, however, come to guard Agnes and the other lost items. They were there to guard the heavy locked canvas bags which held all the money collected at subway change booths during the past twenty-four hours.

At eight o'clock the next morning, the canvas bag in which Agnes lay was unlocked. A lost property clerk dumped everything out onto a long table.

The table sat in the center of the lost property office, a strange-looking room lined with steel shelves. One shelf held umbrellas of all colors and sizes. Another shelf held briefcases and books. On another there were thermos bottles and lunch boxes. Still another held bundles of coats, jackets, and shoes. There was a shoebox marked "Gloves." (It also contained two sets of false teeth.) Another shoebox held eyeglasses. A stepladder and a pair of skis leaned against the wall. And standing on the floor were a new red tricycle, a rusty blue bicycle, a statue, a huge lamp, and an ancient upright vacuum cleaner. Each item had a ticket tied to it.

The lost property clerk looked at the ticket which the change-booth man had fastened to Agnes. Then he tied another ticket around her arm. It read:

ITEM 68,301. He wrote out a file card describing the doll. And he put Agnes on a long steel shelf marked "Miscellaneous." There she sat between a portable sewing machine and a toy fire engine with one wheel missing.

All day Agnes sat there. And the next day. And the next. Some of the items were taken from the shelves as their owners came to collect them. But nobody called for Agnes.

Then, on a Monday morning in early April, a lost property clerk took most of the items off the shelves. Everything which had not been claimed for the past six months was to be sold the next day at public auction.

ITEM 68,301—Agnes—had, however, been unclaimed for only two weeks. She could not be put up for sale until the *next* public auction, in October.

Agnes sat, almost alone, on the steel shelf, staring out. She looked very sad, even though she was smiling.

THE LOST-AND-FOUND

Two days later, when Emily got home from school, her mother said, "Well, Em, we're going to Brooklyn. Right now."

"Now?" Emily wailed. "I'll miss all my best programs!"

"I'm sorry, but I may need you," her mother said.

"*Need* me?" Emily exclaimed. "For *what?*"

"You'll see. And by the way, Em—bring your library card."

They took the subway, changing trains two times. Finally they got off and climbed a flight of

48

stairs. Then they entered an office with black words written on the door. Emily didn't trouble to read the words. They looked too big.

"Where on earth *are* we?" she asked as they walked into a large, empty room. It had blue walls and a counter, with no one behind it. There was, however, a small bell with a sign: *Please ring*.

Emily's mother rang.

A lost-property clerk in a blue uniform came from a back room.

"I'm Mrs. Ellison," Emily's mother said. "I phoned this morning. I've come to identify Item 68,301."

The clerk nodded. Went to the back room. And returned with Item 68,301.

Emily stared.

Then she screamed.

And she shrieked,

"Agnes!"

"Well," said the lost-property clerk, "I guess that identifies the doll all right!" He handed Agnes over the counter.

Emily clutched her rag doll. "Agnes! It's YOU!"

Her mother and the clerk watched her. Both were smiling. "It's moments like these," said the lost-property clerk, "that make this job worth a lot more than what they pay me."

Finally, Emily stopped prancing and dancing and kissing her doll. She looked at her mother, tears sliding down her cheeks. "Mom, how on earth did you find out that Agnes was *here?*"

"I didn't," said her mother. "I phoned up and described her. They said they had a rag doll, but all rag dolls look pretty much the same. I didn't want to raise your hopes for nothing. We couldn't be sure it was really *Agnes* until we got here."

"Where are we, anyway?" asked Emily.

"The Transit Authority's lost-property office. I got the idea last night, watching the news on TV. They showed an auction of things lost on subways and buses."

"But I *didn't* lose Agnes on a subway or bus!"

"I know," said her mother. "That's why we never thought to call here before."

"Matter of fact," said the lost-property clerk, "we get all kinds of items in here. Lost in all kinds of places. But not many people realize that. So they never bother to phone us."

"Oh, Agnes," Emily exclaimed, hugging the doll hard. "I never *really* thought I would ever find you again!"

The clerk pushed a card over the counter. "If you'll just sign this, young lady."

Emily looked at the yellow card. It read: ITEM 68,301. *Rag doll. Hair: Brown (wool). Eyes: black (buttons). Height: 11 inches. Clothing: red gingham dress.* It also noted the place the doll had been found. The date she had been found.

And at the bottom there was a name:

Miss Ida M. Pickering
485 West End Avenue
New York City 10024

"Who's *that?*" Emily pointed to the name.

"The person who turned Agnes in." said the clerk. "If you hadn't called, then after six months we'd notify Miss Pickering. If *she* didn't want Agnes, the doll would be sold at the next public auction."

"Did Miss Pickering bring Agnes all the way out here to *Brooklyn?*" Emily asked.

"Nope," said the lost-property clerk. "That wasn't necessary." And he told her all about the change-booth man, and the lunch-relief man, and the dispatcher.

"Do you mean," Emily exclaimed, "that all those people went to all that trouble over *my* doll?"

"Well, she's quite an important item," said the clerk. "Anyone can see that." Then he pointed at the yellow card. "Now sign right here. And show me some official identification."

Emily signed her name. And showed her library card for identification.

"Could I have *Agnes'* identification card?" she asked.

"Afraid not," said the clerk. "We need this for our records."

"Well," said Emily, "could I copy off the address of the lady? I want to write and thank her."

"Sure thing," said the clerk. "I know that Miss Pickering—whoever she is—will be glad to hear you two got together."

"Maybe Agnes and I will go thank her in person," Emily said. Carefully, she copied the name and address of Miss Ida M. Pickering. Then she looked up. "Can I take Agnes home now?"

The lost-property clerk nodded, and cut the identification tag from Agnes' arm. "Seems to me," he said, "this is one mighty happy-looking rag doll."

"Well," said Emily, "she really loves me an awful lot. Don't you, Agnes?"

The doll looked back at Emily with her black-button eyes. And she smiled.

About the Author

Peggy Mann is the author of many books for young readers, including *The Street of the Flower Boxes*, which has been made into a film for television. Her books for adults include *A Room in Paris* and *Golda: The Life of Israel's Prime Minister*. She has also written articles and fiction for most of the major national magazines.

Miss Mann lives in New York City with her husband, William Houlton, and their two young daughters, Betsy and Jenny. Betsy's loss of a beloved rag doll inspired the story of *The Lost Doll*. Although Betsy never got her doll back, Miss Mann was fascinated by the workings of the city's little-known "lost-and-found machinery," and was delighted by the concern shown by officials for "so small an item and so small a child."

About the Illustrator

Thomas di Grazia studied at Cooper Union in New York and at the Academy of Fine Arts in Rome, Italy. He has illustrated numerous books, both juvenile and adult. In 1972 his work for a Hallmark book of poetry won a Society of Illustrators Award. Mr. di Grazia lives in New York City with his wife and two children.